DEVIL'S DONKEY

Devil's Donkey

by Bill Brittain
drawings by Andrew Glass

HARPER & ROW, PUBLISHERS

NEW YORK

Cambridge
Hagerstown
Philadelphia
San Francisco

1817

London
Mexico City
São Paulo
Sydney

Devil's Donkey

First Edition

Library of Congress Cataloging in Publication Data
Brittain, Bill.
Devil's Donkey.

SUMMARY: Dan'l Pitt doesn't believe in magic
until he comes up against Old Magda the witch.
[1. Witches—Fiction. 2. Magic—Fiction]
I. Glass, Andrew. II. Title.
PZ7.B78067De 1981   [Fic]   80-7907
ISBN 0-06-020682-9
ISBN 0-06-020683-7 (lib. bdg.)

J
B

For Knox and Dorothy—my parents—
who always cared

Chapters

even know what it was. Maybe he'd get sick . . . even die!

Meanwhile, the boy must have found a chunk of wood with a knot in it, as I heard him shouting out there.

"Log, you'll split if it's the last thing I ever do!" *Thunk.* "Think you're tougher'n me, huh?" *Thunk.* "Of all the dang-blast . . ."

WHOOSH

A sudden gust of wind shook the whole store and sent dust devils whirling up and down the street outside. I thought it odd that a wind would come up like that on such a clear day. But there's no explaining New England weather.

"Dan'l!" I called. "Come in here."

HEE HAW!

I couldn't believe my ears. Dan'l was mocking me, making strange sounds.

Mad or no mad, he couldn't get away with that. I ran out the door and around the side of the store in nothing flat.

"See here, Dan'l Pitt, I don't care if you are sore about . . ."

And then I was brought up short.

Because Dan'l wasn't to be seen anywhere.

In his place by the woodpile, with its ears standing straight up on its head and its tail sticking out stiff from its body like it was scared to death, was a *donkey*.

CHAPTER TWO

At Old Magda's

At first seeing that donkey I thought Dan'l might be having a joke on me. It wouldn't have been the first time.

It wasn't as if the donkey could have wandered into my backyard by itself. The yard had a fence around it, and the gate was locked. Yep, another of Dan'l's pranks, I thought.

And then I saw something on the ground, right beside that critter's off foreleg.

A little pile of clothes. Pants and a shirt and shoes and underwear and socks. The socks were white.

And one of 'em had a spot of blood on it.

Dan'l's clothes. Had the boy run off all naked?

Suddenly I got to shivering and shaking all over. What I was thinking was . . . was impossible. And yet . . .

Talking real soft so that donkey wouldn't kick out at me, I hunkered down by its right hind leg. I felt of the hair just above the hoof, and when I looked at my fingers, there was blood on 'em.

That animal had a cut in just the same place the Coven Tree had scratched Dan'l's leg.

I examined the beast closely. It was a donkey, all right. Kind of gray-brown all over. But its eyes were wide with fright, and they appeared more human than donkey. I began talking to the critter, man to man. Or in this case, man to donkey.

"Dan'l Pitt, is this Old Magda's spell? Is this here donkey really you?"

HEE HAW! HEE HAW!

The donkey brayed and pounded its hoofs on the ground and nodded its head all at the same time.

For a moment I was struck speechless. "It appears you can understand me just fine, Dan'l," I said finally. "Can you talk, too?"

HEE HAW!

"This is awful! You're just lucky I was near when you changed. A person who didn't know better would figure you wasn't nothing but a dumb animal. And you wouldn't be able to tell 'em different."

What appeared to be tears began running out of Dan'l's eyes and soaking into the hair that covered his long head. I never in my life saw such a forlorn-looking creature.

"Old Magda said she'd get recompense for you chopping limbs from the Coven Tree," I said, shaking my head. "And she's done it for fair.

Though turning you into a donkey seems a mite extreme. What we have to do now ain't going to be pleasant. But it's necessary."

The donkey cocked his head like he didn't quite know what I was getting at.

"We've got to go see Old Magda," I explained. "Somehow I have to talk her into removing the spell."

HEE HAW! HEE HAW!

I could see Dan'l didn't want anything more to do with Old Magda.

"We've got to. Otherwise you could be a donkey for the rest of your life. You wouldn't want that, would you?"

HEE HAW!

Dan'l swung his big donkey's head back and forth, saying "no" in the only way he could.

I decided we'd best not head for Old Magda's shack down by the bog until after supper. That way she'd have the whole day to consider the terrible thing she'd done. By the time we set out, there was a dirty pile of storm clouds above the hills to the west, and I wore my slicker against the coming rain. Dan'l'd just have to get wet. I didn't have anything in the store big enough to keep rain off a donkey.

I rode on Dan'l's back. Seemed more natural that way. On my arm was a basket filled with canned goods and chocolate bars. A few gifts to soften Old Magda's heart.

Her shack at the edge of the swamp looked so dank and dismal it might have been something risen from out of the mud. But smoke was coming from the chimney and a candle shone in the window. I tied Dan'l to a tree in front and walked to the door.

It creaked open before I could knock. "Come in, Stew Meat," Magda's voice called. "I've been expecting you."

She was bending over a pot on the stove and stirring something with a long wooden spoon. In a corner of the low ceiling a spider had spun a network of web, and an owl perched o' the cupboard was staring at me with eyes as cold as death.

HOO!

"Quiet, Hecate!" snapped Magda. "Sit down, Stew Meat. There, by the window."

I started shivering, partly from the cold drafts blowing through the cracks in the walls, but mostly from pure fright.

Magda finished at the stove and shuffled to a chair made of a huge hogshead. "I brought you some things," I said by way of starting.

"Bah! Don't try to soften me up with gifts. You're here about Dan'l Pitt."

"Course that's why I'm here. Now I'm willing to admit the boy did wrong. He offered you insult and . . ."

"Boy? What's this talk of a boy? The only Dan'l Pitt I know is a donkey."

"Consarn it, Magda, he didn't cut the limbs off the Coven Tree to plague you. He just doesn't understand our ways."

———

"Of course not, Stew Meat. A donkey doesn't have to understand anything. It only has to pull and haul and do whatever its master desires."

"Magda, don't go making light of the fix you got Dan'l into. Imagine being trapped in a donkey's body all day."

"A day? A single day? Ha! Dan'l Pitt will live out the rest of his time in Coven Tree as a beast. And when he's taken from this village, it will be as a donkey still."

I didn't like the sound of that. "I . . . I didn't know Dan'l was planning on leaving us," I said slowly.

Magda's eyes glittered, as cold as river ice. "His plans are the ones I make for him. Know, Stew Meat, that the moment Dan'l Pitt's blood was shed beneath the Coven Tree, his body became my property, to shape and dispose of as I wish. And I choose that the boy be a donkey."

"You can't!" I shouted. "Dan'l's near to being a man, and he has the right to live as a man."

Outside, there was a rumble of thunder and

a flash of lightning. Then the rain started pelting down, sounding like lead shot dropping on the roof.

"Dan'l forfeited his rights when he cut into the wood of the witches' tree," Magda snarled. "For the present, if you like, you may keep the boy-beast at your store and treat him as human or donkey, whichever pleases you. But know, Stew Meat, that by and by Mr. Beel will come to Coven Tree. Maybe in a week or perhaps not for several months. But long ago I pledged to Mr. Beel that I would deliver to him a donkey. And Dan'l Pitt will fulfill that pledge."

"Mr. Beal?" I said. "The only Mr. Beal I know is a flagman down at the depot."

"This Mr. Beel spells his name with two e's," Old Magda told me. "He's a traveling man—a collector of sorts. This year it's donkeys he's wanting."

"You'd sell Dan'l to a horse trader? Look, if it's money you need . . ."

"No!" Old Magda tossed her head and folded

her arms. "I cannot sell to you. The boy's already promised to Mr. Beel."

I felt my heart sinking inside me. If Old Magda was set on selling Dan'l to that Beel fellow as just another donkey, sell him she would!

But I wasn't ready to give up yet. I'd been a Yankee storekeeper forty years in New England, where a man who can't talk his way into a shrewd deal or out of trouble doesn't last long.

Just maybe I could trick Old Magda into showing me how to make Dan'l human again. Then she'd never sell him to a horse trader.

"If Dan'l's to remain a donkey, it's a pity," I said. "But before he's taken away, I might as well get some work out of him. With him hitched to my wagon, I could deliver groceries right to people's doors. I reckon folks'd be willing to pay a little extra for that."

"That's right," cackled Magda. "Work the boy hard."

"But there's no chance he'd change again by accident, is there? I mean, I'd hate to be going

---

up a steep hill and suddenly find the wagon rolling back on me with a boy in harness instead
of a donkey."

She shook her head. "The spell's powerful.
Just be careful not to say . . ." And then Magda
put her hand to her thin lips. "You're a clever
one, Stew Meat. But I'll never give away the
magic words."

I tried to look ashamed of her outsmarting
me. But inwardly I was real proud.

Words would break the spell. And I thought
I knew the words. The last lines of Old Magda's
chant went through my head.

> *"Then let the magic spell be cast*
> *When Dan'l Pitt next says . . ."*

I hadn't heard the end. But whatever it was,
it had to rhyme with "cast."

And what were Dan'l's last words out by the
woodpile? "Of all the dang-blast . . ."

Dang-blast. That'd fetch Dan'l back.

I couldn't wait to get that boy—eh—donkey back to the store. With a fast good-bye to Old Magda, I was out the door and down to the tree where he was tied.

With the rope wet from the rain, the knot I'd made was hard to untie. My fingers kept slipping, and I was scared and at the same time mad at myself for being so clumsy. Finally I said the thing that was foremost in my mind.

"Dang-blast!"

WHOOSH

A mighty gust of wind. And at the same time, a flash of lightning.

And there was Dan'l, with the donkey's bridle hanging loose over his red hair, and naked as a plucked chicken. I threw my slicker over him, and we splashed off down the path to the main road.

But from her window, Old Magda had seen Dan'l change. As I ran through the puddles along the path, with Dan'l well out ahead of me, the door of the shack flew open, and Old Magda shouted into the darkness.

"You tricked me, Stew Meat! But you and Dan'l Pitt haven't seen the last of my spell. Know of my anger and be afraid!"

I was afraid, all right. All that long run back home, with the rain streaming down, I was about sick with worrying what kind of deviltry Old Magda would be up to next.

Once we reached the store and got into some dry duds, though, I wouldn't have been human if I hadn't put a question to Dan'l.

"What was it like? Being a donkey, I mean?"

Dan'l's face got real pale. "It was awful, Stew Meat," he said with a shudder. "It's a scary thing to have to stand on four legs when you're used to standing on two. And I had that long head with my eyes and big floppy ears at one end and my mouth way down at the other, and that tail drooping out behind me. I never did get that tail working proper. And instead of hands, I had big clumping hoofs and . . . and . . ."

"Take it easy, Dan'l," I said. "You're back to being a boy again."

"But the worst thing was not being able to call for help. All I could do was bray. When you had me standing out front this afternoon, I tried to tell people the fix I was in, but all that came out of my mouth was . . . was . . ."

And then he burst into bitter tears. "I don't ever want to be a donkey again, Stew Meat," he sobbed.

"That's why we've got to be extra careful from now on," I told him. "Old Magda wants you to be a donkey so's she can sell you to some traveling horse trader. A fellow named Beel. But you're safe as long as you're a boy.

"O' course, Magda'll be madder'n ever after the way she was tricked tonight. So keep a sharp eye out. And if you see her coming, you git! Run off to where she can't find you and you can't hear her."

"I'll be real careful." Then he grinned

through the tears. "Old Magda can't witch me if she can't catch me."

And off he went to bed, all happy at being a boy again.

Me, I stayed up most of the night, feeling like there was a lump of lead in my stomach. For I knew if Old Magda searched for Dan'l, she'd find him.

CHAPTER THREE

Caught !

The days went by, and we kept waiting for Old Magda to make her next move. But as the days turned to weeks and there was no sign of her, I got to feeling better. By the middle of July I'd pretty well convinced myself the whole thing was over and done with. The way I saw it, she'd finally come to her senses and realized the awful thing she'd done to Dan'l just on account of a few dead branches. Maybe she was just too ashamed, I thought, to come around and say she was sorry.

Which just goes to show how little I knew about Old Magda's real plan for Dan'l. Being a witch, Magda was an expert at playing the waiting game.

Some parts of this story—like this next— aren't anything I saw for myself. I had to put them together from listening to people talk afterward.

I had a trip planned to New York City, and I'd been looking forward to it all year. Two full weeks with nothing to do but order my line of winter clothes and get some hardware in. Course, I planned to see the sights, too. There's all kinds of grand things in New York City. And since Old Magda was keeping to herself, I saw no reason not to go.

Dan'l, of course, would stay behind to tend the store.

So I guess it was mostly my fault when he

got himself in a peck of trouble. For I never gave a thought to how, except for Old Magda, I was the only one in Coven Tree who knew how Dan'l got himself changed.

I caught the Saturday evening train to Boston. The next day being Sunday, I figured the boy'd have a day of rest before having to handle all the business by himself.

As soon as he'd churched, Dan'l planned on doing a little fishing. He knew a private spot on Spider Crick where the willows hung right over the water, shading it from the sun. And a little after noontime, he was sitting at the edge of a deep pool, dangling a hookful of worms in the water and hoping a big trout was hungry for lunch.

The day was warm, and the breeze soothed Dan'l's spirit. In the store he was always on the lookout for Old Magda, but away off here in the woods he could just relax for a few hours. With a contented sigh he snuggled against a tree trunk.

HOO!

Dan'l looked up. High above the network of tree limbs, a bird with spread wings soared in the blue sky. An owl.

Strange. Owls didn't usually fly during the day. They were night birds. Uneasily Dan'l remembered me telling him about Hecate, the owl Old Magda kept for a pet. But this couldn't be the same one. Just a bird that happened to wake up a bit early and was hungry.

HOO!

The owl folded its wings to its body and fell through the air like a black meteor. Then, just above the tree where Dan'l was seated, the bird spread its wings to slow its descent. Delicately it perched on the topmost branch.

For a long time boy and bird stared at each other. Then Dan'l's neck started to ache from being tilted back so far. He blinked and looked at his bobber, floating motionless on the water. His eyelids felt heavy, and he closed them.

It was half an hour later when Dan'l woke.

The owl was still above him in the tree. But now it seemed to be looking off toward the far side of the stream at a blackberry bush that Dan'l couldn't remember being there before he'd fallen asleep.

Then the blackberry bush began to shimmer and tremble and change its shape. Dan'l frowned and rubbed his eyes and wondered if he was seeing things. Even as he did so, the bush turned into a figure, standing at the bank of the crick and staring at him.

"Old Magda!" shouted Dan'l in alarm. He set himself to get up and run. But the witch waved her hand, and he became still as a rock. His mind shouted, "Move!" but his body couldn't obey. All he could do was watch helplessly as Old Magda waded across the crick toward him. As she stepped out of the water and onto the bank, Dan'l was amazed to see that neither her shoes nor the bottom of her long cloak had been dampened by the stream.

The witch looked down at him. "Why don't

you call Stew Meat to help you as he did last time?" she cackled.

Dan'l tried to cry out, but even the smallest sound was impossible. He could only wait for what Old Magda was about to do.

"Dang-blast!"

WHOOSH

As the witch uttered the spell, a fearful blast of wind bent the willow trees. Dan'l felt that same awful twisting of his bones and churning of his flesh that he'd felt the last time he'd changed.

And instead of a boy, there was a donkey on the bank of Spider Crick, struggling to its feet and getting untangled from a little pile of clothes. Beside the animal, Old Magda sank to the ground and sat with her head bowed, gasping for breath.

"So tired . . ." she groaned.

Quick as he could, Dan'l went to say the words that'd change him back. "Dang-blast" was the thought in his head. But what came out of his mouth was something else again.

HEE HAW!

Dan'l stood there on his four legs, scared to death. Here he was, stuck at being a donkey, and the only person who knew the words that could change him back was out of town for two weeks.

Old Magda had bided her time and picked the perfect moment to recapture Dan'l.

Slowly the witch got to her feet. She shook her head as if trying to collect her thoughts. "Such strong spells should be left to the younger witches," she mumbled. "I'm too old . . . too old. . . ."

She blinked her eyes and shook her head. "Now what mischief was I about? I keep forgetting. . . ."

HEE HAW!

"Dan'l Pitt, to be sure. Quiet, you foolish beast."

With a shaking hand, Old Magda drew from her cloak a piece of cord braided of what looked like snakeskin. She looped the cord about Dan'l's donkey neck and tied the ends tightly. "Stand easy now," she ordered.

Much as Dan'l wanted to run away, he was powerless.

"While the cord circles your neck you'll do anything you're told," said Magda with a sneer.

Dan'l thought how easy it'd be for a boy to untie the magic loop and cast it away. But in his donkey's body, that was impossible.

"Come along now, donkey." Old Magda hobbled off through the woods, and Dan'l was forced to follow.

Pretty soon the woods opened up into a meadow. Beyond that were some fields with potatoes and corn growing, and off in the distance a farmhouse with smoke coming from the chimney.

"Hello, the Binghams!" shouted Old Magda as she and Dan'l drew near the house. "Come and see what I've got for you."

The back door opened and a man came onto

the porch. His clothes were ragged and patched, but he was powerfully built. Yet Dan'l could see the fear in his eyes as he looked at the witch.

"We've . . . we've done nothing to bring down your witchcraft on us," he said in a trembling voice. Then he called back through the open door. "Anna! Anna, it's Old Magda."

The woman who came outside had a stick of wood clutched in her fist. "There'll be no mischief here, Magda," she said, shaking the stick menacingly. "If you so much as raise a hand to begin one of your spells, I'll give you the drubbing of your life."

"I come in friendship," said the witch. "I brought you something."

And then the girl walked out of the house. She was about Dan'l's age, and the prettiest thing he'd ever seen. Her hair was the color of corn silk, all shiny from lots of combing, and she had eyes as blue as the sky and a mouth that was made for laughing.

"Stand there by your mother, Jenny," said the man.

Jenny—Jenny Bingham. Dan'l remembered seeing her down in the village just that winter. Only then she'd been all wrapped up in scarves and a hat that hid about everything but her eyes. He wished he'd gotten a better look at her then.

"What did you bring us, Old Magda?" asked Jenny.

"This." And the witch patted Dan'l on the neck.

"A donkey?" said Jenny's pa. "But . . ."

"What devilish business are you up to now, Magda?" asked Anna Bingham, her eyes flashing angrily. "What would a witch want in return for a gift like this?"

"Oh, dear me, the donkey's not a gift," said Old Magda. "Call it a loan if you like."

"A loan?" Mr. and Mrs. Bingham looked at each other, puzzled.

"Yes. You'd really be doing me a favor. The

donkey's mine, but I have no use for it right now. If you were to keep it here, I'd know it was stabled and fed proper. And you can work it, hard as you want. The more work, the better."

Anna Bingham cocked an eye at Dan'l. "Well . . ." she said doubtfully, "if you're sure we wouldn't be obligated. The beast would be a help getting those stumps pulled and the corn cultivated. And next spring we'll . . ."

"No," said Magda with a shake of her head. "You may keep the animal for now. But there'll be a day when Mr. Beel comes to town. And on that day you must give up the donkey."

"Oh, Pa," said Jenny. "Even if the donkey's here for only a little while, there's so much it could do. Please let it stay."

"I dunno," replied Mr. Bingham, scratching his head. "It just don't seem right somehow. I'm still not sure . . ."

"Maybe we're being just a bit *too* suspicious of Old Magda, Paul," whispered his wife. "Perhaps she does just need a place to keep the animal. And all the hard work around here is wearing the three of us down. If it comes to a choice of one of us pulling the cultivator or letting the donkey do it, I vote for the donkey."

"Wellll . . . all right," said Mr. Bingham. Jenny's delight lit up her face.

"The beast will follow your orders so long as the cord stays tied about its neck," said Old Magda. "So you must never take it off. And another thing. Always keep the donkey here on the farm, and don't let a soul know you have it. I won't be plagued by having everybody in Coven Tree asking to borrow him. Let this be our little secret."

HEE HAW!

At last Dan'l saw Old Magda's plan. If nobody knew he was being kept on the Bingham farm, there was no chance he'd ever become a boy again. Everybody'd think Dan'l Pitt had just run away, and nobody'd even come looking for him. For the rest of his life he'd be just a dumb, four-legged critter, fit only to haul wagons and pull a plow and live in a stable.

And what would happen on the day Mr. Beel came to town? Who was Mr. Beel, anyway?

"Nobody'll find out from us that we're keeping your animal," said Mr. Bingham.

Dan'l groaned. But the Binghams thought the donkey was just making animal noises.

As Old Magda went off down the path to the main road, Dan'l could hear her cackling laughter. "Jenny," said Mr. Bingham, "go tie that animal in the barn."

Jenny brought a leather strap from the house and fastened it to the cord around Dan'l's neck. Meekly he let himself be led off to the barn, where Jenny put him in a stall. Then she gathered a big forkful of hay from the loft and placed it in front of him.

"Critter, I know you can't understand a word I'm saying." Jenny caught her breath in a kind of sob. "But I'm hoping that Mr. Beel never comes by these parts. Doing the hauling and plowing and weeding and all with just our own hands is wearing us down, Ma and Pa and me. So please be with us awhile. We need you."

And then she kicked the side of the stall angrily. "What foolishness, talking to a dumb animal. I'd best go start supper."

And off she went.

Dan'l bowed his head sadly. When Jenny had talked to him, his heart had gone out to her. He'd be happy to help on the farm, he wanted to tell her. But not as a donkey.

He was human. Human!

HEE HAW!

CHAPTER FOUR

At the Binghams'

The next morning Dan'l stood in his stall, his ears drooping sadly. He hadn't had much sleep, as he couldn't get used to being trapped in his donkey's body. Once he'd even tried to stand up on his hind legs, only to trip and fall heavily to the floor. And how he wished he had hands and feet instead of the hoofs that were so awkward and heavy.

Through the little window of the barn he

51

could hear the Binghams at their breakfast in the house. Mr. Bingham told a joke, and his wife and Jenny laughed merrily. The smell of pancakes reached Dan'l's nose and made his mouth water. He chewed at a mouthful of the hay. It didn't taste bad—a little like salad. But Dan'l wanted human food. He wanted to talk and sing and laugh and do all the things people did.

But here he was, living in the barn, with nobody for company but Primrose, the Binghams' cow. All Primrose did was chew her cud and wait patiently until milking time came. That might be all right for her. She wasn't nothing but a cow. Dan'l, though, was a . . . a . . .

He was a donkey. And for the rest of his life, that was all he was ever going to be. Laughing and singing and talking and dancing and the thousands of other joys that set people above the animals were all gone—gone forever.

A big fly buzzed about the barn. Finally it landed on Dan'l's flank. The fly bit him savagely, and it hurt. Like a bee sting. Dan'l struck at the fly with what should have been his right hand. But his donkey's foreleg wasn't jointed properly for him to reach the offending fly. As the pain increased, he kicked out with a hind leg, missing the fly but giving himself such a blow to the ribs that it knocked the breath out of him and brought tears to his eyes.

The fly bit deeper.

And then, with a slight flick of his hindquarters, he brought his tail around and brushed the fly away. A tail was a handy thing, he realized—for a donkey.

The big door behind him creaked, and Jenny came into the stall. "Sun's up, critter," she said. "Time to get to work. There's five acres of corn to cultivate today."

She took the harness and a big, padded horse collar from a hook just outside the stall. She pulled the collar over Dan'l's head and worked it down to his shoulders. Next, the traces—the wide leather straps that would pull whatever he was hitched to—were fastened to the collar.

Finally Jenny grasped Dan'l at the sides of his mouth. She was stronger than he'd thought, and the pinching fingers hurt. He opened his mouth, and Jenny slid the iron bit into the gap behind his teeth.

When the bridle was buckled on, Dan'l found himself harnessed and ready for the day's work. He felt awful foolish with all those straps draped over him. "Giddup," ordered Jenny with a shake of the reins. And off they went toward the cornfield.

The cultivator had long iron teeth that went deep into the ground to root out the weeds. Dan'l wondered if he'd have the strength to pull it. But as soon as he tried, he found his donkey's body had more strength than five humans.

He dragged the cultivator through the brown earth with no more trouble than a human would have pushing a baby carriage. Up and down the rows of corn he went, with Jenny following behind to guide the cultivator and see it didn't cut off any cornstalks. "Critter," she said once when they stopped for a rest, "you sure know your stuff. Most donkeys would have stomped at least a few of the stalks. But you slide between the rows like a hot knife through butter."

It pleased Dan'l to know that if he had to do a donkey's work, at least he was doing it right.

Late in the afternoon, when the cultivating was finished, Mr. Bingham came to the stall and gave him an extra portion of oats. "It's good having you here, critter," he said, smiling. "If we had to do all that cultivating by ourselves, it'd take the better part of a week."

Dan'l bowed his head. It was hard, seeing the Binghams so happy when he was so miserable.

And so two weeks went by. Each morning Jenny would harness Dan'l, and he'd be set to work hauling the stone boat or pulling stumps or hitched to the hay wagon. And each night he stood in his stall, his human soul grieving for its lost body.

He thought sometimes of running away. He even tried it once when Jenny led him into the barnyard before putting the harness on. But he'd taken only two steps when Jenny ordered, "Whoa, critter." The cord about his neck did its magic, and he stood without moving, meek as a kitten.

Jenny found an old saddle in the barn, and one Sunday she strapped it onto Dan'l and climbed up on his back. Off they went, as she guided him through the woods to a secret spot she knew where Spider Crick widened to form a pond. She got off and gathered some wild daisies while Dan'l grazed nearby. It was shady and cool, and Jenny sang to herself while picking the flowers. Then she sat down under a tree to plait them into a long ribbon.

"Oh, critter," she said, looking at Dan'l, "I wish there was somebody I could talk to. Someone my own age. I get so lonely out there on the farm. 'Specially the summers, when there's all the work to be done and little time to go to town."

She stopped, almost as if she expected Dan'l to answer her.

HEE HAW!

She went on, talking about the wonder of growing up, and how scary it was at the same time. And she spoke of the awful, grinding tired that gathers deep in the bones when farm work is more than three people can manage, and the soft gentleness of sitting before the fire of an evening, with a kitten purring in her lap and the kettle at the boil. There was the terrible winter when Mr. Bingham had taken sick, and the glad time three weeks later when his fever had finally broken. And all the hopes and plans and dreams that she held deep in her heart and didn't speak of to anyone and wouldn't be talking about now if there was anybody listening except a funny-looking donkey.

And Dan'l looked in her eyes and longed to

tell her of his own dreams—dreams Old Magda had turned to dust.

"Critter," Jenny said finally, "if I didn't know better, I'd allow you understood every word I said."

Dan'l wondered what Jenny would say if she knew who she was really talking to.

That evening a neighbor dropped by in a battered pickup truck to take Mr. and Mrs. Bingham to choir practice. From his stall, Dan'l could hear Jenny humming in the house as she cleared away the supper dishes.

How Dan'l longed to be able to talk to her and ask her help. Furious at what Old Magda had made of him, he kicked at one of the boards at the front of the stall. Take that, you witch, he thought.

His hoof thumped against the wood and left a little mark.

ᴗ

For a minute Dan'l just looked at the mark.

Then he kicked at the boards again. A little lower, this time.

ʊ

Inside the house, Jenny heard the donkey kicking at the stall time after time. "What's that fool beast trying to do?" she asked herself. "Knock the barn down? I'd best go out and see what the trouble is."

Once inside the barn, she didn't dare enter the stall, where Dan'l was still banging his front hoof against the boards. Instead, she walked into the oat bin and peered over its wall to the stall beyond.

At first she kept her eyes on the donkey, covered with lather and striking out with its hoof.

And then she saw the marks on the forward wall of the stall. They seemed to make letters . . . words!

DANG BLAST

"He's writing something. . . ." Jenny could scarcely believe her eyes. "It says 'Dang-blast'!"

WHOOSH

The roaring blast of wind threatened to blow the barn down. And there stood Dan'l in the stall, looking at his fingers and toes like he'd never seen anything so wonderful before.

In the oat bin, Jenny covered her eyes with her hands and started screaming fit to bust.

"Oh! Oh, you . . . whoever you are. I never thought I'd see the day . . . Put something on yourself!"

Dan'l realized he wasn't wearing anything but a piece of cord tied about his neck. He yanked it loose and threw it away.

"Jenny Bingham," he said, getting red in the face, "you'd better keep your hands over your eyes. I just got back from being a donkey for two weeks, and I didn't bring any clothes with me."

"But how could . . ." For a moment Jenny

was caught up in the surprise of it. But then, with her hands still covering her eyes, she stumbled her way out of the barn.

"You wait here," she called back to Dan'l. "I'll get you . . . I don't know. Something."

A bit later, Dan'l heard the back door of the house creak open again, and then footsteps coming toward the barn. In the moonlight he could just make out Jenny's arm reaching in the barn door and dropping something in a little pile. "Here, Mr. Donkey-Man," she said in a kind of whisper. "These clothes belong to Pa, so they might not fit proper. But at least you'll be covered. Then come in the house. It appears to me you've got some explaining to do."

A few minutes later, sitting by the stove in the kitchen, Jenny heard Dan'l's feet on the back steps. "Come in, Donkey-Man," she called through the door. "I'm the only one at home. Our talk will be private."

Dan'l entered the kitchen and sat down.

"You've been calling me 'critter' while I was a donkey," he said. "But my real name is Dan'l Pitt."

Jenny looked at him solemnly. And then a smile broke across her face that gladdened Dan'l's heart. "Was . . . was it really you in that donkey's body?" she asked. And then she giggled. "Those floppy ears. And that tail . . ." And then ripples of laughter took the place of words. "All so . . . silly! A donkey. It . . . it's so *funny!*"

"It wasn't funny to me," said Dan'l sternly. But then the joy of being human again overcame him, and he found himself laughing right along with her.

Finally the laughing ended. Jenny spoke in a low voice. "How . . . how did it happen, Dan'l?"

He told her the whole story. From chopping the branches off the Coven Tree to kicking the words into the stall so Jenny could release him from the spell.

They were both quiet then. Finally it was Jenny who spoke.

_____

"Dan'l?"

"Yes, Jenny?"

"What'll you do now? I mean, if Old Magda discovers you've turned back into a boy, won't she . . . ?"

"She won't trouble me anymore. Soon as I can gather up my things at the store, I'm running far away. Maybe down to Boston. Old Magda will never find me there."

Jenny looked at him and sighed. "I'll miss you, Dan'l," she said. "You've been the closest thing to a friend I've had all summer, even when you were a donkey."

Dan'l got red-faced and flustered. "It's too dark to find my way to town tonight," he said. "If there's someplace I could bed down . . ."

"The barn," Jenny replied. "And you'd best be off by first light before anybody's about. It'll be hard enough explaining to Ma and Pa how old Magda's donkey got away, without them seeing *you* here, too."

Dan'l nodded and took up a lantern from

the shelf. "Pleasant dreams, Jenny Bingham," he said.

"Pleasant dreams to you, Dan'l Pitt," she answered. "I . . . I'd be pleased if you'd write me a letter when you get to . . . to wherever you're going."

"I'll write, Jenny. Soon as I get settled."

Up in the barn loft, with the sweet-smelling hay all about him, Dan'l stared solemnly into the darkness. Running away—it was a big step. He'd miss the town of Coven Tree. He'd miss the store, and the folks who came to buy, and the country way of doing things and . . . and . . .

. . . And he'd miss Jenny. Consarn that Old Magda and her mean tricks anyway!

Through the little opening at the peak of the barn, Dan'l heard a fluttering of wings. And then there was a sound that brought out goose bumps all over his body.

It was the single cry of an owl.

HOO!

CHAPTER FIVE

A Donkey Again

I was some riled up to get home from my trip and find the store hadn't been open while I'd been away. And when I finally did open up the following morning, still rubbing the sleep out of my eyes, there was Dan'l on the front porch.

"You got more brass than a pair of cymbals, Dan'l Pitt!" I bellered at him. "Running off the way you done."

"Just hear me out, Stew Meat. Please."

Mad as I was, I guessed I owed him a chance to tell his side of things.

When he got done, I was still mad. But it wasn't Dan'l I was mad at any longer. It was Old Magda.

"So I've got to run off, Stew Meat." Dan'l was having a hard time holding back the tears. "If Old Magda was to change me again, I . . . I don't know what I'd do."

"Yeah, I reckon it's for the best," I told him. My own eyes got watery, and I gave 'em a swipe with my handkerchief and then blew my nose loudly. "Let's just hope Old Magda's power don't reach as far as Boston."

It didn't take us long to get Dan'l's things together. I put 'em in my best suitcase, and when the boy wasn't looking I slipped in two twenty-dollar bills.

We stood by the front door for a minute, just looking at each other. I had a lot of things I felt like saying by way of good-bye. But the words just wouldn't come.

"I guess everything will work out for the best," I told Dan'l finally. "In spite of Old Magda's spell."

Speak of the devil and up he'll jump, goes the old saying. And I guess it works for witches, too. For when Dan'l turned to go, there was Old Magda standing in the doorway.

"My owl, Hecate, brought me a strange message last night," she said in a kind of croak. "She said there was a donkey up at the Bingham place that had changed into a boy. This morning that same boy ran past my place on the way to the village. I came to see for myself if you'd escaped from my spell again, Dan'l Pitt. And it seems you have."

I looked from Old Magda to Dan'l. The boy's face was white as a fish's belly, and his mouth kept opening and closing with no words coming out. It wasn't right, I thought, that anybody— even a witch—could put so much fear into another person's heart.

"Consarn it anyway, Magda!" I said. "Dan'l's

been punished thrice over for cutting those limbs from the Coven Tree. Let him be!"

"Not yet, I think," she cackled. "For when Mr. Beel comes by, he'll be expecting a donkey. And a donkey he'll get."

"Magda, if money means that much to you, I'll pay whatever . . ."

"Money?" Old Magda waved her hand, and a little pile of gold coins appeared on the counter beside me. "I spit on your money. Who needs it?"

Another wave of her hand, and the coins vanished.

"If you change him," I told her, "I'll just change him back."

"Will you?" she snarled. "We'll see about that. But first things first."

She turned to Dan'l, who was cowering in a corner. "Dang-blast!" she cried.

WHOOSH

The rush of wind coming in through the door set Old Magda's cloak to flapping about her scrawny body. And when the wind let up, there was the donkey, standing in the corner where Dan'l had been.

I opened my mouth to say the words to change him back. But Old Magda, who was slumped against the wall and breathing heavily, managed to raise a trembling arm and level a crooked finger at me.

The words stuck in my throat. My mouth kept flapping, but nothing came out.

Tired as she seemed to be, Old Magda wouldn't be able to keep me quiet for long. I figured to just wait until she left. Then I'd change . . .

"Now buy the best . . ." Old Magda started. Then she stomped her foot in annoyance. "No! The words are wrong. Oh, why can't I get things to stay in my mind anymore?"

It looked to me like Old Magda was getting set to crank up still another spell. If she didn't do herself real harm in the process.

"Now boy is beast . . . Yes, that's it!"

From somewhere Old Magda summoned up the strength to stagger to the open door. She spread her arms wide, and it almost appeared she was embracing the whole village of Coven Tree.

*"Now boy is beast, and you will find
The magic spell gone from your mind."*

For a long moment she just leaned against the door, all tuckered out and looking as pale as death. Me, I didn't know if I was more worried or surprised. For I'd never seen Old Magda this way before, so sickly and forgetful. Time was when she could work any spell she wanted, easy as rolling off a log. But now . . .

I'd never thought much before about witches dying. And if Old Magda passed away, what would become of Dan'l then?

"Something more . . ." she wheezed. "Something more I must do. But I forget. . . ."

Slowly she turned to me. "My spell won't

last forever," she rasped between deep breaths, "upon those who've not shed blood by the Coven Tree. But I reckon this one will work until next the mists come down from the mountain, and dogs howl, and the hair of cats stands on end as they claw at things unseen. When that time comes, Mr. Beel will visit Coven Tree. And when he leaves, the donkey will leave with him."

And then she vanished through the doorway.

Once she was gone, my voice came back. I turned to the donkey. The expression on the poor beast's face was saying, "Get me out of this fix, Stew Meat," just as sure as if Dan'l had spoken the words aloud.

So I tried.

"Dad-blum!" I said, loud and clear. But there the donkey stood, waiting impatiently. I had another go at it.

"Gosh-durn . . .

"Dag-nabbit . . .

"Golly-shucks . . ."

I couldn't remember the changing words! Old Magda's new spell had chased them clean out of my head.

HEE HAW!

Dan'l started in braying and stomping his hoofs on the floor and carrying on fit to bust.

"Oh, Dan'l," I said in a shaking voice. "I've forgot what to say to change you back to a boy. Old Magda done that to me. We're in a peck of trouble now."

As soon as Dan'l heard that, there was a clatter of hoofs as he headed for the door. It was kind of a tight fit for his donkey body, but finally he forced himself through, and the last I saw, he was galloping past the blacksmith shop and out of town.

"Dan'l!" I called after him. "Where in tarnation are you . . . ?"

But I knew where he was headed.

Jenny Bingham was the only person left who'd be able to change Dan'l into a human again. If she failed, he'd be a donkey forever!

And then something peculiar came into my head. I thought about that pile of coins Old Magda had witched onto the counter. And about her saying how we'd know when Mr. Beel was coming.

The blood in my veins seemed to turn to ice water. For if what I was thinking was true, being a donkey was the least of Dan'l's troubles. I reached under the counter and pulled out the Bible I kept there.

And after reading a few pages of it, I could do nothing else but sink to my knees and pray that Jenny Bingham would be able to remember the words that would make Dan'l Pitt a boy again.

Dan'l found Jenny out in the barn. She was staring into the stall where he'd lived for two weeks, and she was shaking her head in amazement. "The words Dan'l kicked into the wood," she was saying to herself. "They're gone. I wonder if Pa . . ."

But Dan'l knew it wasn't Mr. Bingham who had polished the boards to a high shine. It was Old Magda's doing. Part of her spell.

And now that donkey was really worried. HEE HAW!

Jenny turned about, seeing him for the first time. "Dan'l?" she asked, puzzled. "Is that you?"

HEE HAW! HEE HAW!

Jenny saw at once how scared Dan'l was. "Now don't you worry a bit," she said comfortingly. "I'll just change you right back."

She led Dan'l into the stall and then went off into a far corner of the barn, remembering that when he changed, Dan'l wouldn't have any clothes on. "Sock-dollager!" she called out confidently. Then she turned her head, expecting to see Dan'l grinning at her over the side of the stall, happy at being a boy again.

HEE HAW!

"It . . . it didn't work!" she gasped. "I must have said the wrong thing by mistake."

"Sam Hill! Thunder-ation! Ding-bust!"

Time after time she tried, but nothing came out right.

Finally, her shoulders slumped and head bowed, she shuffled back to the stall. "It's no use, Dan'l," she moaned. "My head's all awhirl. The words aren't in it anymore."

Dan'l's heart sank. He tried desperately to think of the changing words in hopes he could kick them into the wood again. But they were gone from his mind, too.

"Oh, Dan'l!" Jenny threw her arms about his neck and hugged his donkey head close to her own. Tears were streaming down her cheeks.

"I'll always be your friend, Dan'l," she sobbed into one of his long ears. "That won't change, even if you *are* a donkey. But I know how much you want to be a boy again, and now everything's just . . . just terrible. What's to become of you, Dan'l?"

Even if he'd had a voice, Dan'l wouldn't have been able to answer that one. He just didn't know.

CHAPTER SIX

Mr. Beel

I never did open the store that day. The hours went by, and I couldn't do anything but wring my hands and worry about Dan'l's fate once he fell into Mr. Beel's clutches. The sun reached its zenith and then descended toward the western horizon, and still I could think of nothing that would save him.

As the late afternoon shadows lengthened there was just one little seed of an idea in the back of my mind. But it needed time to take root and grow. I saw the mist gather about the tops of the mountains as it does every summer evening, and I thought that perhaps tomorrow when my mind was fresh I'd be better prepared to . . .

Off in the distance a dog howled. And then I watched in horror as the mist settled down among the forests of the mountainsides. It appeared almost solid, gliding and coiling and letting its tendrils slide among the trees like a nest of white snakes. Downward toward our valley it came. Ever downward.

Just outside my window, the firehouse cat snarled and spat at something no human eye could see.

And I knew that for Dan'l Pitt there might be no tomorrow. If he were to be saved, it would have to be tonight.

I set off toward the Bingham farm at a dead run. Twice I fell, skinning my knee and turning my ankle so it ached fiercely at every step. As

I limped on, the howling of dogs echoed throughout Coven Tree.

The sun had almost set by the time I arrived. I found Jenny in the barn, forking down hay for Dan'l. Her eyes were red as she turned to me.

"Stew Meat!" she said, surprised. "But why . . . ?"

"No time!" I gasped. "Come, Dan'l. We must see Old Magda."

Reluctantly, Dan'l came out of the stall. But Jenny grasped his bridle, and he was still.

"I don't understand," she said. "Dan'l's scared and hungry. Whatever you want, can't it wait until . . ."

"No!" I cried. "It can't wait. For Mr. Beel is coming tonight. And we must see Old Magda before he arrives."

Jenny's face was white, and her eyes were wide. But there was no denying her courage. "Dan'l will go to Old Magda's only if I come, too," she said. "For he's helped my family these past weeks, and now I'll help him if it's in my power." And she gripped the bridle rein more tightly.

"Come along, then!" I shouted.

A candle burned in the window of Old Magda's shack when we got there. Leaving Dan'l, Jenny and I scrambled to the door and pounded loudly.

"Come in."

As we opened the door, Old Magda rose to greet us. There was a wide grin on her withered face.

"Come to bargain again for Dan'l Pitt, have you?" she said with a gloating laugh. "You're too late. For tonight, Mr. Beel comes to collect Dan'l for his own."

"And that's been your purpose all along, Old Magda!" I cried. "I knew when you conjured up the gold coins in my store this morning that you had no need to sell Dan'l for money. You deal in something far more valuable."

"Purpose?" asked Jenny timidly. "What purpose, Stew Meat?"

"Magda's power comes from the Devil himself," I replied. "And the Devil gives nothing away free. There must come a time when a witch pays tribute to her master. She must make an offering of some kind. And Dan'l Pitt is Old Magda's offering."

"But how . . . ?"

"When Dan'l shed his blood beneath the Coven Tree, Old Magda saw her chance. She had power then to change his body. She made a donkey of him as a sign that he was her tribute to Satan."

"Shrewdly spoken, Stew Meat," said Old Magda with a chuckle. "And there's nothing you can do to save the boy."

"The Devil will not have Dan'l Pitt!" I roared.

"No? And how would you prevent it? He's my property now, to dispose of as I will."

"Perhaps, Old Magda. But when Mr. Beel

comes to take Dan'l, he'll find you don't own that property free and clear."

"Not own him free and clear?" Magda glanced about wildly, as if searching for something she'd lost . . . or forgotten. But then she sneered at me. "Ridiculous!"

"Shall we put the question to Mr. Beel himself?" I asked.

For a moment she trembled like a frightened animal. But then a shrewd glint came into her eyes. "And if your argument doesn't hold merit, Stew Meat, there's a price to be paid. A very high price."

"I know that. And still I would look Mr. Beel in the eye and have my say. I need only your promise that whatever happens, Jenny Bingham will not be harmed."

"She will be safe," agreed Old Magda. "But I cannot say the same for you and Dan'l Pitt."

We arrived at the Coven Tree about ten minutes before midnight. Old Magda and I both carried lanterns that gave a feeble light and turned the limbs of the old oak into monstrous shadows. Jenny held tightly to Dan'l's bridle.

A minute passed. A second and a third. Throughout Coven Tree the dogs' howls and the cats' shrill cries rang out like a chorus of lost souls.

And then the noise stopped. The silence was like a muffling blanket, something you could almost touch.

Dan'l heard it first. His long ears stood upright on his donkey's head. And then the sound came to the rest of us, soft but clear through the misty dark: the jingle of harness and the creaking of wooden wheels too long ungreased.

Up the road came something that was at first only a blackness darker than the night itself. Then the gypsy wagon groaned its way under the limbs of the Coven Tree and into the lantern light.

The wagon was a dirty red, the color of dry blood. Two darkened windows were set deep into

---

each side like the eye sockets of a skull. Thick black smoke boiled from a stovepipe that angled out from the roof.

The wagon was pulled by two donkeys, and a third was tied behind. At each plodding step the beasts made little moaning noises deep in their throats that could have been pain or terror—or both.

But it was the wagon's driver that held us spellbound.

Set close against each side of the hawk's beak of a nose, his eyes glittered in the light and the flames of hell danced in them. His mouth was twisted into a cruel smile that revealed long, pointed teeth, and there was a stubble of beard on his chin.

He wore a wrinkled suit of checkered wool, curiously old-fashioned, with a stiff-collared shirt and a string tie. A hat with a high curl to its brim was on his head, and his boots were misshapen, as if the feet inside were of a form other than human.

As he turned toward me, he seemed to be peering into my very soul.

"Mr. Stew Meat, I believe?" he said in a whispery voice. "Mr. Beel, at your service."

By now I was quivering inside, but I'd be blamed if I'd show him how scared I was. "Mr. Beel?" I questioned. "Is that the name you take now?"

"Oh, I have many names," he said calmly. "Old Nick . . . Lucifer . . . and here in New England, Mr. Scratch is quite popular."

"Yet whatever name you take, you are still Beelzebub, whom the Good Book calls the prince of the devils!"

He laughed hideously, and behind me I heard Jenny gasp and Dan'l's hoofs patter against the earth. "You have found me out, sir." He climbed down from the wagon seat, and when his boots touched the ground, steam arose from the damp earth. "But my business is not with you, nor with the pretty young lady there . . . at least for the present."

He turned to Old Magda. "Have you brought the tribute which I demand?" he asked sternly.

"Yes, master." She came forward fearfully, like a puppy who doesn't know whether or not its owner will give it a beating. "See. The donkey that stands by the girl. It waits only to do your bidding."

"Then I'll just tie it to the wagon and be on my way," said Mr. Beel. He reached for Dan'l's bridle.

"Wait!" I cried out. "For that's not just a donkey you'd take with you, Mr. Beel, as you well know. That is a human boy who's been witched into the form of a beast. And neither you nor all your demons shall take him from Coven Tree!"

"This is a straight business deal between Old Magda and me," said Mr. Beel. "I hardly see where you enter into it, Stew Meat."

"I speak for that donkey—for Dan'l Pitt—because Old Magda has no right to give him to you."

"No right?" cried Old Magda. "I have every right. For the moment Dan'l Pitt put ax to this tree, his body was mine to do with as I would."

"True," I agreed. "You have control of Dan'l Pitt's body. But what of his soul?"

Now it was Magda and Mr. Beel's turn to be surprised. "Yes, Dan'l Pitt took wood from the witches' tree," I went on. "But that's no sin, except in the mind of a witch. So Magda turned him into a donkey to deliver him up to you, Mr. Beel. But you may not take him, because his soul remains unstained by evil."

For a moment Mr. Beel just stared at me. Then there came a sound as of great stones grinding together, which was the angry gnashing of his teeth. Menacingly, he turned to Old Magda.

"A bargain must always be struck," he snarled at her. "Wealth, good fortune, a pleasing appearance, or some other small and unimportant thing in return for . . . You made such a bargain for the boy's soul, of course?"

"N . . . no, master," Old Magda answered in a timid voice. "There was no time. After Stew Meat tricked me into . . . And then the girl saw the words in the stable. . . . I had all I could do just . . ."

"Stop sputtering excuses, old crone!" In his rage, Mr. Beel shook his fist at the sky, and heat lightning flickered along the horizon. "I can see beyond your petty lies."

"But master . . ."

"You simply forgot, and that's the whole of it. Even as a girl, three hundred years ago, you were absentminded. I thought you'd grow out of it. But as you become old and feeble you forget that the only way I can gain souls is by appealing to human greed. You act as if your brain has turned to dust!" Mr. Beel stomped his foot angrily. "By all that's unholy, can I find none but fools to serve me?"

Old Magda seemed to shrink within herself in the face of Mr. Beel's wrath. But then her mouth twisted into an evil leer. "Take the donkey-boy as he is now, master," she wheedled. "Once he's in your kingdom, you'll have all eternity to gain his soul. He'll give it up gladly in return for . . ."

"Have you lost your mind completely?" roared Mr. Beel in a voice of thunder. "No one who is pure of soul may enter my domain. And the soul goes with the body. Since I cannot take the one, I may not take the other. But you'll pay for this mistake, you wretched hag. I promise you that!"

"I beg you, Mr. Beel . . ." But he turned his back to her.

"This is most embarrassing, Stew Meat," he said humbly. "Recently Old Magda has made a number of small errors in my service. I was able to overlook them, but this is unforgivable. She must be punished. As for myself, I assure you, I simply assumed Dan'l Pitt was like the others."

"What others?"

He spun about, pointing to the donkeys harnessed in front of the wagon. "That one on the left was the strongest woodsman on the whole Kennebec River. He bargained for money. The other was a Bangor politician. He bargained for power. And the one tied on behind was once a fine lady. She bargained for beauty. Now they're mine. But Dan'l Pitt made no bargain, so he will stay in Coven Tree. A pity, too. He'd have made a fine addition to my stable."

"But . . ." I hardly dared ask the question. "Is Dan'l to remain a donkey forever?"

"Long years ago I gave witches the power to change those who harmed their trees," said Mr. Beel. "And I cannot revoke it. So whether Dan'l Pitt is donkey or boy is up to her. And from the anger I see in her now, my guess is he will stay as he is."

So we'd met the Devil and bested him, and hadn't gained a thing. Dan'l was still a donkey.

And then an evil smile split Mr. Beel's face, and his eyes glowed. "Unless . . ." he began.

"Unless what?"

"I'm a creature who likes a good wager, Stew Meat. If we were to make a bet—and if you were to win—I'm sure I could talk Old Magda into making the boy human again."

"Stew Meat, no!" Jenny had come up behind us, still grasping Dan'l's bridle. "You can't make a bet like that. Not with the Dev— with him!"

I looked unsurely at her and then back to Mr. Beel. "What kind of a bet did you have in mind?"

"Umm." Mr. Beel eyed Dan'l up and down. "That's a fine strong critter you've got there. D'you think he could outpull my beast?"

He pointed at the off donkey of his team— the one that had once been the strong woodsman.

"Don't do it," pleaded Jenny. "Please, Stew Meat."

And then I felt Dan'l tugging at my sleeve with his teeth. I turned and he started nodding his head up and down. Make the bet, Stew Meat, he seemed to be telling me.

"I don't know, Dan'l . . ."

HEE HAW!

Dan'l nodded harder'n ever.

"I'd hear your terms, Mr. Beel."

"Very well. Your Dan'l will be harnessed back to back with my animal. They pull against each other until one of them drags the other backward across the center line. The one who outpulls the other wins."

"Where and when?" I demanded.

Mr. Beel shrugged. "Tomorrow noon, perhaps? In front of your store?"

"With Dan'l Pitt's soul as the wager, eh?" I asked.

"No, Stew Meat." Mr. Beel's voice was a snake's hiss. "The winner takes *all!*"

And his knobby finger pointed straight at me.

My tongue glued itself to the roof of my mouth, and I felt like somebody'd let the air out of my innards. If Dan'l lost, I'd be sharing his fate. I could feel sweat popping out on my fore-head.

"You . . . you'll use no magic or witchcraft?" I asked, stalling for time.

Mr. Beel shook his head. "Just two donkeys pulling against one another."

A part of me kept wanting to call the whole thing off. But that was the coward's way. And it'd be dooming Dan'l to live out the rest of his life as a donkey. There are times when a man has to do what he thinks is right, without count-ing the cost.

"Mr. Beel?"

"Yes, Stew Meat?"

"It's a bet."

CHAPTER SEVEN

The Pulling Contest

Leaving Mr. Beel and Old Magda at the Coven Tree, Dan'l and Jenny and I stumbled our way back to the store with only our lantern to light the way. Once there, Jenny stabled Dan'l while I called up the Binghams, knowing they'd be worried to death about Jenny being out so late. I made up a story about how she was helping me balance my account books and we'd lost all track of time. The lie sounded pretty weak to me, but I could tell from Paul Bingham's voice on the phone how relieved he was. I couldn't help wondering how the Binghams would feel if I'd told 'em what we were really doing.

After showing Jenny to Dan'l's room above the store, I settled into my own bed. Not that I was in the mood for sleep. I was so scared and jittery I sat bolt upright every time I heard a board creak. All I could think of was how tomorrow we'd be battling the Devil himself. And the prize would be our very souls. All night long I called myself six kinds of a fool for making that bet with Mr. Beel. Barring a miracle, I figured Dan'l and me would both be leaving town soon, trotting on four legs and tied to the Devil's wagon.

It was about five in the morning, with a false dawn showing along the horizon, when I nodded off to sleep.

One thing you get used to in a small town is everybody knowing your business almost before you know it yourself. With the ladies gossiping over back fences and the gents doing the same thing down at Jed Hooper's barber shop, and then everybody going home and passing along the latest news over the party-line phone, there's no such thing as privacy. In Coven Tree it's like living your life in a big window with the whole village looking on.

So it wasn't surprising that I was woken up around eleven by the sound of a crowd of people murmuring to one another. I looked out my window, and it seemed like everybody in Coven Tree was gathered in front of the store. Word of the contest had gotten out somehow. I suspected Mr. Beel had something to do with it. Maybe he wanted the whole village to see me and Dan'l brought low. I doubted, though, that he'd told anybody who he really was.

I rubbed the sleep from my eyes, dressed, and went to the kitchen, where Jenny had already prepared a big breakfast. After we ate, we went out the back way to the barn to harness up Dan'l.

When it was done, Jenny took a little hand-kerchief from her pocket and tied it to the bridle strap. "For courage," she told Dan'l. "And for luck."

HEE HAW!

I got to say this about the boy. His braying sounded a lot more confident than I felt.

We followed Dan'l out into the sunlight. As he came around the front corner of the store, a big cheer went up from the crowd. They gathered around, and a few even stretched out hands to pat what they thought was just another donkey.

"Splendid animal, Stew Meat."

"Where'd you get him? Looks real strong, he does."

"Ain't no other donkey in the world that can outpull a Coven Tree critter."

There was some betting going on, too. I was gladdened to hear the odds were favoring Dan'l.

And then a littler murmur went through the

crowd. Everybody turned, looking off down the road.

Mr. Beel was coming.

Only now he appeared a lot more human than last night. The evil glitter was gone from his eyes, and his teeth weren't all pointed anymore, and his boots fit proper. He might have been just some traveling peddler passing through town.

But it was the donkey he was leading that caught most folks' attention. It looked even stronger than I remembered. Its muscles bunched and stretched and gleamed in the sunlight like its whole body had been rubbed with oil. Even its harness shone like polished steel.

There were little whispers from the crowd, and some people who'd put money on Dan'l in the early betting were looking mighty worried.

Mr. Beel walked straight up to me. "Good day, Stew Meat," he said. Then he stuck out his hand to me.

I jammed my own hands deep in my pockets. Mr. Beel didn't own me yet. And I wasn't about to shake hands with the Devil.

Jenny stuck out her tongue at him.

"I hope you don't mind my spreading the word about our contest," he said with a chuckle. "I thought a crowd urging the beasts to do their best would add excitement to the occasion. Of course, I never mentioned the terms of our bet. Now then, are you ready?"

"Don't be in such a consarn hurry," I grumbled. "First off, we need to pick a judge."

"Mayor Tubbs is quite acceptable to me," replied Mr. Beel. "He's usually called on for events like this, I believe."

I found Farley Tubbs, and he acted suitably surprised when I asked him to judge the contest. But he was carrying a piece of thick rope with him all the same.

I looked about, kind of surprised at not seeing Old Magda anywhere. "Remember your promise," I whispered to Mr. Beel. "No magic."

"No magic," Mr. Beel agreed. "You have my word on it."

The two donkeys were stood tail to tail. Farley tied one end of the rope to the traces of Dan'l's harness. The other end was knotted to the harness of Mr. Beel's donkey.

I couldn't take my eyes off the beast. It was bigger and heavier than Dan'l, and its muscles stood out like thick slabs of oak under its skin. I couldn't honestly see that Dan'l had a prayer of outpulling such an animal, and I felt fear grip my heart.

I thought Jenny'd like to be right close when the pulling started. But to my surprise she slipped off into the crowd.

"May I have the names of your animals?" asked Farley, full of his own importance.

I hadn't counted on Dan'l's needing a name. But I couldn't let on who my donkey really was. "Uhh . . . Donkey-Boy."

"My animal is called Hercules," said Mr. Beel.

"Ladies and gentlemen!" Farley bawled. Everybody got quiet. "This here pulling contest is between Donkey-Boy, belonging to Stew Meat . . ."

A few people started in cheering. I figured those were the ones who hadn't been able to switch their bets to Hercules.

". . . and Hercules, Mr. Beel's animal!"

A lot of cheering then, from all the folks who'd bet against Dan'l.

Mr. Beel and I led the two donkeys apart until the slack in the rope was taken up. Then I stood to one side, as did Mr. Beel.

I couldn't help wondering what people would say if they knew the devilish wager at the heart of this contest.

Farley took a stick and scratched a line in the dirt directly betwixt the two donkeys. "First animal to drag the other across that line—all four feet—wins!" he announced.

And then he started counting, pulling his arm down at each count like he was yanking on a bell rope. "One . . . two . . . three . . . PULL!"

Neither donkey needed any urging. Hercules kind of threw himself against his collar, and I saw Dan'l rear legs start to buckle. But then he recovered, and the two donkeys stood like statues, all four hoofs of each planted solid, and that rope between 'em stiff as an iron bar.

"Pull, Donkey-Boy!" shouted somebody in the crowd. And "C'mon, Hercules!" yelled someone else.

And then I saw Dan'l start in quivering all over. The boy was beginning to weaken. But it was happening a lot faster than you'd expect in a healthy donkey. There was something odd going on.

I heard an angry shout. I turned about to see Jenny striding across the road. She was clutching a stick of stove wood in one fist, and her face wore a scowl that didn't bode well for whoever she was mad at.

She marched right by the straining donkeys.

She'd seen something I only now noticed.

A bramble bush at the edge of the road, its thorny branches waving and twisting in the breeze.

Except there wasn't any breeze.

"I thought you'd be lurking about somewhere with your mischief!" Jenny cried. "You stop witching Dan'l this instant!"

With that, she hit the bush a couple of good licks with her stick.

"Oww!" And suddenly it wasn't a bush anymore, but Old Magda standing there with both hands upraised, all ten fingers hooked like claws and pointing straight at Dan'l.

At Old Magda's shout, Mr. Beel turned around. When he saw what the witch was doing, his face began to slide and change and become terrible to look upon. His eyes were no longer those of a kindly peddler but the eyes of a panther, glittering evilly. His nostrils flared like an angry bull's, and his pointed wolf's teeth champed together with a loud sound. Warm as the day was, I felt a chill blast of wind at my back, and Old Magda shivered and trembled with fear.

"You would dishonor me, old crone?" snapped Mr. Beel, and Old Magda seemed to shrivel before his gaze.

"But, master . . ." she sputtered.

"Have done, madam!" roared Mr. Beel. "I gave my word there would be no magic in this contest. And I will not have you make a liar of me. For there's more deviltry in the truth, when told for evil purposes, than in all the lies in the world."

"I only thought . . ."

"And what a fine mess your thinking has made of things up to now! From here on, just do as I say. No more magic in this contest, Old Magda. I command it."

Then Mr. Beel turned to me, and his face was again that of the peddler. "I crave your pardon, Stew Meat," he said humbly. "Old Magda exceeded her authority—another of her bad habits."

With Old Magda taken care of, Dan'l's strength returned with a rush. But Hercules already had the advantage. Slowly Dan'l was pulled backward. He was reaching a point where he'd have to shift his hoofs, and as soon as he tried that, Hercules would have him pulled across the line before he could get set again.

THUNK

Both donkeys went plunging away from each other. Dan'l nearly ran into a tree before he could stop himself.

"The rope broke!" shouted a man in the crowd.

Nobody'd ever seen a rope break in a pulling contest before. There was some talk about calling the whole thing a draw.

"What do you think, Dan'l?" I whispered into one of his long ears. "Do we accept a draw and let things stay as they are right now? I mean, that Hercules is one powerful critter."

Deep down I was hoping he'd say yes. But he shook his head back and forth, and I knew he was set on seeing things through to the end.

"Donkey-Boy will pull again," I announced. And Mr. Beel nodded his agreement.

"Fetch a chain," Farley ordered. From the store I got a length of chain an elephant couldn't bust. The donkeys were positioned and the chain fastened to the traces.

I glanced over at Jenny. She had Old Magda well in hand. Whichever animal won would do it fair and square.

"One . . . two . . . three . . . PULL!"

Dan'l's rear hoofs slammed against the earth like hammers. His shoulders leaned into the padded leather of the collar, and the length of chain became rigid. He felt the muscles of his legs flex and push. It seemed that Hercules just had to move.

But there was just the steady strain on the

lines. Dan'l felt like he was trying to pull the whole state of Maine.

His chest heaved, and the air came burning into his lungs. The cheering of the crowd was drowned out by the roaring in his ears. He felt the muscles in his hindquarters tighten up, and he knew he couldn't go on pulling much longer. The strain was too much.

He had been a fool to let the bet be made. Hercules would win and then . . . what?

And by losing he'd doom not only himself. He'd be delivering me into Mr. Beel's clutches, too.

Suddenly Dan'l understood what it would be like never to be human again. And as hard as his donkey's body was striving, he found himself thinking on all the things he'd be forsaking. The simple pleasure of talking to Jenny and being able to touch her with his words. The warmth of rich earth trod by bare feet, and the sleepy comfort of dozing in front of a fire when the wind blew raw outside. The tang of cold cider on a hot day, and the fluffy softness of a kitten's fur, and the miracle of watching a tiny seed grow to fullness in the sun and rain. All the joys of being human, the joys no animal could know.

These were the things he'd lose today. They and all the glory and wonder of simply being human.

And Dan'l pulled. All his heart was in the pulling, and his whole donkey's body seemed filled with renewed strength. For he was pulling to save his soul.

Then, incredibly, he was moving. Ahead. And the crowd was cheering.

Dan'l looked behind him.

The donkey Hercules was down on its hindquarters, with forelegs stuck out straight like a sitting dog. Beside the animal knelt Mr. Beel, shaking his fist angrily.

But Mr. Beel's anger came too late. Beyond him was the line in the earth across which Hercules, struggling and braying, had been dragged.

Dan'l had won!

———

CHAPTER EIGHT

A Boy Again

I patted Dan'l's hairy flank. "Well done, sir," I said proudly.

And then I heard an outraged cry behind me. I spun about to see Jenny marching toward me with Old Magda in tow. Jenny had a tight grip on Magda's cloak and was almost dragging the witch. Old Magda was whooping and hollering fit to bust. It was all she could do to stay on her feet, never mind working any spells.

"Change Dan'l back!" Jenny ordered. "He won fair and square, so you make him a boy. Right now!"

"No!" Old Magda shook her head. "He deserves to remain a donkey. And you can't make me change him, Jenny Bingham."

Jenny looked at me in despair. And then Mr. Beel approached us. "Congratulations, Stew Meat," he said. "You win . . . for the present. But perhaps we'll meet again. And now, if you'll excuse me . . ."

"You just hold on here," I told him. "A bet is a bet. You promised Dan'l'd be a boy again. Now Old Magda's saying she won't make good on that promise. I tell you now, Mr. Beel, if you don't honor the bet you made with me and Dan'l, there won't be a place in New England where you'll ever be able to make another. We don't hold with bad losers."

Mr. Beel looked sharply at Old Magda, and in his eyes was a hellish anger. "Old Magda keeps forgetting who is the master and who the servant," he said harshly. "I won't have her defy me. Why, if her attitude were to spread to the other witches . . ."

He began muttering something to Old Magda. The words he spoke were in a language I'd never heard before, but from the scared expression on Old Magda's face, she understood them all too well. By the time Mr. Beel finished lecturing her, it looked to me like she was going to have troubles of her own from now on.

"Old Magda will remove the spell," Mr. Beel told me. "And I'm going to teach her a lesson in obedience she won't soon forget. Now I must be on my way. I have some . . . eh . . . collections to make."

He walked off, taking Hercules with him. That donkey was limping something awful.

I looked expectantly at Old Magda. "Well?"

"D . . . dang-blast," she said reluctantly.

WHOOSH

We all turned our backs to the strong gust of wind, and when we looked around again, there was Dan'l the boy. He was peering at his arms and legs and rejoicing at being human once more. You could see how grand he felt after all that time in a donkey's body.

At first, folks were struck dumb by the change. One moment, there stood a donkey, and the next, the donkey had become Dan'l Pitt. A few people blessed themselves, and others wrinkled their noses at the stink of brimstone in the air.

Then somebody chuckled. You couldn't blame him. Dan'l did look mighty funny, standing there without any clothes on, with his head sticking up through that horse collar and struggling to free himself from the harness straps. Before long the whole crowd was roaring with laughter.

"Get me some pants!" Dan'l howled. More laughter. "Get me something to cover myself with, dang-blast it!"

When we heard *that*, both Jenny and I caught our breaths. But nothing happened. The

changing words didn't work anymore. The spell was broken, and Dan'l was free.

Farley Tubbs found a blanket to cover Dan'l. At the same time I looked about for Mr. Beel. I wanted to tell him the next time he came around "collecting," he could just pass Coven Tree by.

But I was too late. For Mr. Beel had already left. When last I spied him he was far down the road that led to the witches' tree, taking the donkey Hercules to its awful fate.

"Master! Mercy, master. Please!" Old Magda cried after him. But Mr. Beel paid her no mind. And for the first time in the three hundred years that she'd been the Coven Tree witch, tears glistened in Old Magda's eyes.

And so the story of how Dan'l Pitt was changed into a donkey comes to its end.

Yes, Dan'l Pitt still clerks in my store. And if any newcomer to Coven Tree starts scoffing at our traditions—especially the ones that concern witches—Dan'l sets him straight in a hurry.

The boy's taken to spending a lot of his time helping out at the Bingham place, too. The crops are coming along real fine, he tells me, and the Binghams have plans to buy a donkey—a real one.

Then he starts speaking of Jenny, and he gets all red-faced again, and his words come out in fits and starts. He says it's because he doesn't know much about farming, and Jenny always has to tell him how things are done, and that makes him nervous.

But I suspect there's more to it than that.

Old Magda? She's still about. But she's changed a lot since Mr. Beel left town. Her magic spells have gotten to be more of a joke than anything else. Time was, for example, she could conjure up some of the worst storms seen in this county. Nowadays a light drizzle is about the best she can manage. Her owl, Hecate, molted last month, and the feathers never did grow back.

Now that folks don't have to be afraid of

her any longer, they've gotten a lot more friendly. They go out of their way to wish her a good morning, and there's talk of inviting her to join the ladies' sewing circle.

The Coven Tree still stands at the crossroads. And in spite of feeling kindly toward Old Magda, we're all mighty careful when we come near it.

For:

Who sheds his blood by Coven Tree
Under Old Magda's spell will be.

Yessir. Mighty careful indeed.

DATE DUE
